CAVES

DOGS

BENJAMIN HULME-CROSS

Illustrated by
Nelson Evergreen

A & C BLACK
AN IMPRINT OF BLOOMSBURY
LONDON NEW DELHI NEW YORK SYDNEY

First published 2014 by A & C Black,
an imprint of Bloomsbury Publishing Plc
50 Bedford Square
London WC1B 3DP
Bloomsbury is a registered trademark of Bloomsbury Publishing Plc

www.bloomsbury.com

ISBN 978-1-4729-0109-5

A CIP catalogue for this book is available from the British Library.

Printed and bound in India by Replika Press Pvt Ltd

1 3 5 7 9 10 8 6 4 2

The Teens can choose prison for life … or they can go on a game show called The Caves.

If the Teens beat the robot monsters, they go free. If they lose, they die.

I am Zak. Sometimes I help the Teens. Sometimes I don't.

The Teens were called Dan and Jake. They looked strong. They ran to the caves.

The Voice spoke.

"The game begins in 10 minutes."

"Stay with me," said Dan.

"I always stay with you," said Jake. "We both robbed the bank. We both chose The Caves. We will both fight the robots."

"We can do this!" said Dan.

The Teens did a bad thing. But they helped
each other too. That's good.

I took a hammer and a wooden club out of my bag and put them on the ground.

I went deeper into the caves.

I heard the cage door open outside. I heard howls.
It was the dogs.

The Teens ran towards me. They were running away from the dogs.

They had the club and the hammer.

They saw me and they stopped.

"There are two dogs. They will both attack one of you," I said.

"You take the hammer," Jake said to Dan.

"Go into the tunnel!" I said. "Only one dog can chase you in there."

Jake took the club. He went into the tunnel.

I climbed up the walls of the cave.

Dan climbed up after me. He had the hammer.

Two huge dogs ran to the tunnel. They looked wild. They had sharp teeth.

Jake held up the wooden club.

The first dog jumped at Jake's neck but Jake stopped it with the club.

Dan jumped down onto the second dog's back.

The dog howled.

Dan hit it with the hammer.

The first dog bit Jake's leg.

Jake fell to the ground. "Dan!" he called. "Help!"

Dan jumped onto the dog. He hit the dog three times.

The dog fell down. It did not get up again.

Dan helped Jake stand up. They hugged each other.

We heard the Voice.

"Game Over!"

Read more of

THE
CAVES
SERIES

DOGS

DRONE

LION

LIZARD

SNAKE

SPIDER